Sarah-Jane turned around—and jumped back, startled.

She had bumped into the arm of a snowman. It was a beautiful snowman—perfect except that he didn't have a hat.

"What a nuts-o place to put a snowman," Timothy said.

"Why would anyone hide this snowman way down here where no one can see it?" added Sarah-Jane.

"Maybe it's a secret snowman," said Titus. "Like Tim's—"

But he didn't get to finish his thought. From somewhere up above them, an unseen someone began pelting them with snowballs.

"Ambush!" yelled Timothy. "Run for your lives!"

THE MYSTERY OF THE
SECRET
SNOWMAN

Elspeth Campbell Murphy
Illustrated by Chris Wold Dyrud

Chariot Books™
David C. Cook Publishing Co.

A Wise Owl Book
Published by Chariot Books™,
an imprint of David C. Cook Publishing Co.
David C. Cook Publishing Co., Elgin, Illinois 60120
David C. Cook Publishing Co., Weston, Ontario

THE MYSTERY OF THE SECRET SNOWMAN
© 1989 by Elspeth Campbell Murphy for text and Chris Wold Dyrud
for illustrations

Cover design by Steve Smith
First printing, 1989
Printed in the United States of America
94 93 92 91 90 89 5 4 3 2 1

Library of Congress Cataloging-in-Publication Data
Murphy, Elspeth Campbell.
  The mystery of the secret snowman / Elspeth Campbell Murphy;
illustrated by Chris Wold Dyrud.
      p.   cm.—(The Beatitudes mysteries)
  "A Wise owl book."
  Summary: Three cousins explore the mysterious circumstances
around a woman and a quarreling brother and sister, illustrating the
Beatitude "Blessed are the peacemakers."
  ISBN 1-55513-577-3
  [1. Cousins—Fiction. 2. Mysteries and detective stories.
3. Beatitudes—Fiction.] I. Dyrud, Chris Wold, ill. II. Title.
III. Series: Murphy, Elspeth Campbell. Beatitudes mysteries.
PZ7.M95316Mygh   1989
[Fic]—dc20
                                                          89-9758
                                                             CIP
                                                              AC

CONTENTS

"Blessed are the peacemakers,
for they will be called sons of God."
Matthew 5:9 (NIV)

1
BABY'S FIRST CHRISTMAS

Timothy Dawson's baby sister, Priscilla, always got a lot of attention. (Too much, in Timothy's opinion.) But lately Timothy had noticed that the situation was getting even worse. Priscilla was getting more attention than ever. There were two reasons for this.

REASON NUMBER ONE: It was Priscilla's first Christmas. She was born in January, so she had missed last Christmas by a couple of weeks. Now she was almost a year old and as cute as could be. (Too cute, in Timothy's opinion.)

It seemed to Timothy that this year the tree was practically loaded down with sweet little ornaments that said *Baby's First Christmas*. Priscilla had all of Timothy's baby ornaments from years ago, plus tons of her own.

Their cousin Sarah-Jane Cooper had even brought Priscilla a Christmas bib that said *I'm a Little Angel*. Where would it all end?

Sarah-Jane always made a big fuss over Priscilla, of course. But even Timothy's other visiting cousin, Titus McKay, was getting into the act now. That was because of reason number two.

REASON NUMBER TWO: Priscilla was just getting ready to take her first steps. Right now she was doing what the baby book called "cruising." That meant she could stand up and walk around, but she always had to be holding onto something—someone's hand, the couch, the coffee table, the bookshelves.

"Did it happen yet?" Titus kept asking Sarah-Jane. "Did she walk by herself yet?"

And Sarah-Jane, without taking her eyes off Priscilla, would answer, "No, not yet. But anytime now. Priscilla's just the smartest, little baby in the whole, wide world. Aren't you, you little angel?"

That's not what Timothy wanted to say to Priscilla. He wanted to say in his gruffest, Old-West-sheriff voice, "Beat it, Blondie. This house ain't big enough for the both of us."

But he couldn't say that out loud, because his parents were very strict about how brothers and sisters could talk to each other. Of course, Priscilla wasn't talking much at all yet—not unless you counted "muk" (milk) and "kee-coo" (cookie). So she got off easy.

But even if it was "Baby's First Christmas," it was still *Christmas,* Timothy's favorite time of the year. Christmas vacation had just started, and his cousins were visiting for a couple of days, so that was good. Also, Timothy had a fun daily job to do—getting the mail and hanging up the Christmas cards.

Timothy loved the pictures of stars and angels and doves and mangers and the words about peace and joy. In fact, one of the names Timothy liked best for Jesus was *Prince of Peace.* That was on some of the cards.

Timothy heard the mailbox clank open and shut, so he went to do his job.

With all the attention Priscilla was getting lately, Timothy was glad to see a card addressed just to him.

But what he couldn't figure out was why the envelope said *Timmy D.*

No one called him Timmy. Just about everyone called him Timothy—except for his cousins, Titus and Sarah-Jane. They called him Tim, and he called them Ti and S-J.

"That's weird," said Timothy.

"What's weird?" asked Titus and Sarah-Jane eagerly. (The three of them had a cousins detective club, and they always perked up at a possible mystery to solve.)

10

"It's this Christmas card," replied Timothy. "It's weird because of the way the envelope's addressed."

Timothy opened it.

He found out that the card was even weirder than the envelope.

2
THE WEIRD CARD

The front of the card was nice—but kind of babyish. It showed Frosty the Snowman in his big, black top hat. He was smiling as he ran through the streets of town.

Timothy said, "If someone knows you well enough to send you a card, wouldn't that person know how old you are?"

Titus shrugged. "It seems like it. But there's this friend of my mother's who still sends me stuffed bunnies for Christmas. People forget that kids grow up."

Sarah-Jane said, "Ti, if you get another stuffed bunny this year, you should give it to Priscilla."

"Hey, yeah, S-J!" said Titus. "That's a great idea!"

"Can we please get back to my weird card?" asked Timothy.

It turned out that the card was even weirder on the inside. This is what the cousins saw:

Where's Frosty's going
If his big, shiny hat.
Yes, he's coming to see you.
How about that?
For I give him a special job to do.
He's bringing love
From me to you.
Merry Christmas!

"Why is it all marked up like that?" asked Sarah-Jane. "What are all those drawings for?"

13

"I don't know," said Timothy, feeling very puzzled.

"Well, who's it from?" asked Titus.

"I don't know," said Timothy, feeling even more puzzled. "There's no name at the bottom. The person forgot to sign it."

Titus said, "Imagine going to all the trouble of drawing those teensy pictures—and then forgetting to sign the card!"

Sarah-Jane nodded. "It's weird, all right."

3
A SECRET PAL?

Timothy's mother was busy baking Christmas cookies for church, so she couldn't look too closely at the card. But she said, "Maybe someone didn't forget to sign it. Maybe someone left the name off on purpose. Maybe the card is from a secret pal."

"What's a secret pal?" asked Timothy.

His mother explained. "It's when someone you know does nice things for you, like sending you notes and little gifts. Only the person doesn't want you to find out who it is. It's like a kind of game, or a friendly joke."

"Oh," said Timothy. He liked the idea of little presents, but he didn't like the idea of not knowing who sent them.

Timothy often said he liked mysteries. But

what he really meant was that he liked *solving* mysteries. There was a difference. Having an unsolved mystery was sort of like having unfinished jigsaw puzzles or wrapped-up Christmas presents lying around. It drove Timothy crazy.

So he said to his cousins, "I have to get to the bottom of this. I have to find out who sent me this card."

"OK, we'll help you!" said Sarah-Jane. "But where do we start?"

"The postmark!" cried Titus. "At least we can find out where the card was mailed from."

Unfortunately, Timothy had already thrown the envelope away. So they had to dig through the kitchen garbage to get it back. Sometimes detective work could be downright yucky.

But it was worth it.

The postmark on the envelope showed that the card had been mailed from Timothy's own suburb. And there was something even better than a postmark. There was a return address.

Sarah-Jane read it. "*Two-Seven-Nine-Nine Maple Street*. Where's that?"

Timothy was already getting their jackets and boots out of the kitchen hallway. "It's only a couple of streets over from here. Come on, we'll go by the house and see if I know who lives there."

As they set off, Titus said, "I don't get it. If someone doesn't want you to know who sent the card, then why did he put his return address on it? He should know you're smart enough to go to the house and find out who lives there."

"I know," said Timothy, feeling strangely disappointed. "This mystery is going to be so easy to solve. Cinch-y."

"OK," said Sarah-Jane, when they had walked a little way up Maple Street. "The houses on this side of the street are all even numbers—2792, 2794. So we have to cross."

They crossed the street and followed the odd numbers, saying, "2795, 2797. . . ."

Timothy said, "The next house is the one we're looking for—2799."

But there was no next house. Maple Street came to a dead end. And the spot where 2799 should have been was an empty lot.

4
A SURPRISE IN THE RAVINE

The empty lot was actually a little valley—a ravine—with a frozen stream at the bottom of it.

The cousins were astonished to find a ravine where they'd expected to find a house. And, for a moment, no one could think of anything to say.

Finally Timothy said what they were all thinking. "Well. It looks like this mystery won't be so easy to solve after all."

"It's crazy," agreed Titus. "Someone sent you a Christmas card—from nowhere!"

"What do we do now?" asked Sarah-Jane.

None of them was sure what to do next, so they just decided to look around.

They walked single file down the ravine. It

was pretty, but there were no kids playing there. The sides were too steep for sledding, and there were too many trees.

The cousins were busy looking around, when suddenly Sarah-Jane said, "Hey, quit poking me."

"I didn't poke you," said Timothy.

"I didn't poke you," said Titus.

"Well, somebody did," grumbled Sarah-Jane.

Titus said, "You probably just backed into a tree."

Sarah-Jane turned around to look—and jumped back, startled.

She had bumped into the arm of a snowman.

It was a beautiful snowman—perfect except that he didn't have a hat.

"So cool," breathed Sarah-Jane.

"EX-cellent," agreed Titus.

"Neat-O," agreed Timothy. Then he added, "But what a nuts-o place to put a snowman."

"Yeah," said Sarah-Jane. "When you build a snowman, you want everybody to see it. Especially if you did a really good job. So why

would anyone hide this snowman way down here?"

"Maybe it's a secret snowman," said Titus. "You know, like Tim's secret pal. . . ."

"Hey, you know what?" said Timothy. "Except for the hat, this snowman looks just like the one on my card. I wonder—"

But he didn't get to finish his thought. From somewhere up above them, an unseen someone began pelting them with snowballs.

"Ambush!" yelled Timothy. "Run for your lives!"

20

5

THE TWELVE DAYS OF CHRISTMAS

The cousins scrambled back up out of the ravine.

Timothy and Titus scooped up snowballs on the way to throw back at whoever it was who had pelted them.

Sarah-Jane, who positively hated snowballs, had *that look* on her face. It said that the thrower was in for a good talking-to.

But when they got back up to the sidewalk, all they saw was a grown-up lady, walking a dog.

Sarah-Jane was hopping mad. "Where did he go?" she burst out to the lady. "Where's that dumb, stupid kid who was throwing snowballs at us?"

The lady looked a little taken aback. "What? I didn't see anyone."

That was a letdown. Sarah-Jane had no one to yell at, and the boys had a bunch of useless snowballs on hand.

Timothy and Titus hated to see good snowballs go to waste, so they threw them at each other. They didn't throw any at Sarah-Jane. Somehow they knew that would be a Big Mistake.

After that, the cousins didn't know what else to do, so they trudged back home.

"OK," said Titus on the way. "What do we have? Somebody sends Tim this weird Christmas card, with no name. So we check out the return address, only there's no house. Just a ravine. And in the ravine there's this really EXcellent snowman, kind of hidden there. And it looks like the snowman on the card. So—maybe Tim was supposed to find it. But—maybe it was some kind of trap, because—"

Sarah-Jane broke in. "Because some dumb, stupid kid threw SNOWBALLS, and—"

Timothy changed the subject. Fast. He said, "I think we should take a closer look at that card."

When they got back to the house, Priscilla was napping, so they had to be super-quiet. But that wasn't the problem it usually was, because they had some heavy-duty thinking to do.

They opened the Frosty-card again and, for the first time, really *looked* at the drawings.

Sarah-Jane read them off in order. "A person jumping . . . a cow . . . a ballerina . . . a bagpipe . . . a ring . . . a nest with eggs in it . . . a swan . . . a tree . . . a bird . . . a turtle . . . a drum . . . and a chicken. I don't get it. Are the pictures just for decoration? Are they some kind of code? And how can we ever figure it out?"

"What's that on the tree?" asked Titus. "An apple?"

"No," said Sarah-Jane. "It's the wrong shape for an apple. I think it's supposed to be a pear. It's a picture of a pear tree."

As soon as she said that, they all three sat up straight and stared at one another.

Timothy sang softly, " 'On the first day of Christmas, my true love gave to me a partridge in a pear tree.' First day—first *word*?"

"I get what you're saying, Tim!" exclaimed

Titus. "There's a secret message hidden inside the regular message on this card. And the picture for the first day of the 'Twelve Days of Christmas' song shows which is the first word of the secret message. And here's a turtle for the second word!"

"The song doesn't say *turtle*," Sarah-Jane objected. "It says turtle*doves*."

Titus had to admit that she was right, but he still thought Timothy's idea would work. He said, "Maybe turtledoves are too hard to draw. Besides, that song has *a lot* of birds in it. Why would you give somebody all those birds for Christmas? That song is so BOR-ING."

"*Tell* me about it," muttered Timothy. He was in a community children's choir. They gave a lot of concerts in December. And that meant he had to sing "The Twelve Days of Christmas" over and over and over again. But at least he had memorized which goofy present went with which day.

Even so, they kept getting mixed up when they went forwards, so they decided to work backwards, the way the chorus went.

24

Titus got some scratch paper and a pencil.

"OK," said Timothy, after he hummed part of the song to himself. "The twelfth day is 'ladies dancing.' "

"That must be the ballerina," said Sarah-Jane, pointing to the picture. "And she's standing over the word *hat*."

Titus said, "So probably that's the last word in the message." He wrote *hat* in the lower right-hand corner of the paper. That way, he could put the next-to-the-last word in front of it—and so on.

They worked it out so that Timothy said the song. Sarah-Jane found the picture. And Titus wrote down the word.

"Eleventh—lords a-leaping," said Timothy.

"The person jumping," said Sarah-Jane.

The jumper was over the word *Frosty's*, so Titus wrote *Frosty's* in front of *hat*. They noticed that some of the words had been changed a little bit, so he put the changes down, too.

Here is how it went:

"Tenth—drummers drumming," said Timothy.

"The drum," said Sarah-Jane.

Titus wrote down *bring*.

"Ninth—pipers piping," said Timothy.

"The bagpipe," said Sarah-Jane.

Titus wrote down *Yes*.

"Eighth—maids a-milking," said Timothy.

"The cow," said Sarah-Jane.

Titus wrote down *If*.

"Seventh—swans a-swimming," said Timothy.

"The swan," said Sarah-Jane.

Titus wrote down *you*.

"Sixth—geese a-laying," said Timothy.

"The nest with eggs in it," said Sarah-Jane.

Titus wrote down *see*.

They all said, "Fifth—golden rings," since that was the easiest part of the song. The ring was easy to find on the puzzle. Titus wrote down *come*.

They were almost there.

Then they got into a little argument about whether it was "four calling birds" or "four collie birds." No one knew what a collie bird was, anyway. So they stopped the argument, found the bird, and Titus wrote down *I*.

"Third—French hens," said Timothy.

"The chicken," said Sarah-Jane.

Titus wrote down *me*.

"Second—turtledoves," said Timothy.

"I guess that's the turtle," said Sarah-Jane, still not absolutely convinced.

Titus shrugged. "What else is there? We're running out of pictures." He wrote down *give*.

Then they all said together, "First—partridge in a pear tree."

"The tree, of course," said Sarah-Jane.

Titus wrote down *For* and hooked it together with *give*, the way it showed on the card.

When they were all done, they had a message that said:

They didn't know what to make of it at all. Who wanted Timothy's forgiveness? And for what?

"Now the card is weirder than ever," said Timothy. "And we still don't know who sent it."

"There are still some numbers here," said Titus.

After the pictures, solving the number code was a snap. They just put the letters in the order of the numbers. And they came up with the name of the sender. Sort of.

Titus wrote it on the scrap of paper with the message. Here is what the number code said:

your sister

6
WHO IS TIMMY D.?

"My *sister*?!" exclaimed Timothy. "How could it be from my *sister*? Priscilla is the only sister I have, and she's just a baby!"

Titus shook his head in bewilderment. "I'm sure we worked the code right. But there must be some kind of mistake."

Sarah-Jane picked up the envelope and said, "I don't get it. It says right on here, *Timmy D., 2582 Oakwood.*"

"*Oh*-two," said Timothy.

"What?"

"My address is 2502 Oakwood."

Sarah-Jane frowned thoughtfully. "But it says *eight*-two on the envelope."

"Are you sure that's not a zero?" asked Titus.

"No, it's an *eight*," insisted Sarah-Jane. "Because—see?" She opened the card and pointed to the numbers in the code. "This person makes her eights funny. The top loop is too little, so sometimes it looks like there's no loop at all."

The boys saw that she was right. They were all quiet, letting this new idea sink in.

"So—it was all a mistake," said Timothy. "The card was never meant for me at all. I don't have a secret pal. No one is playing tricks on me or setting traps. The card belongs to some little boy called Timmy D., who lives at 2582 Oakwood. I guess we'd better take it to him."

Timothy, Titus, and Sarah-Jane dragged on their jackets and boots. Each one was thinking, "Well, so much for that. . . ."

Suddenly Timothy said something that made his cousins perk up. "But it's *still* weird!"

Titus said, "What do you mean, Tim?"

Timothy said, "OK. This cute, kind of babyish card comes for some little boy called Timmy D. But it says it's from his sister. Why would his sister have to mail him a card?

Wouldn't she live in the same house? And, even if she lives someplace else, and mails him a card, how could he read it? Most little kids can't read at all—let alone figure out a code. And what kind of message is that to send to a little kid? *'Forgive me? I come see you? If Yes, bring Frosty's hat.'* What does that mean?"

Titus said, "The snowman in the ravine didn't have a hat. Could that have anything to do with it? What *I* want to know is, who built the secret snowman?"

Sarah-Jane said, "And what *I* want to know is, who threw those snowballs?"

Timothy said, "And what *I* want to know is, who is Timmy D.?"

They would soon find out. They had been walking as they talked, and now they stood outside of 2582 Oakwood.

"Hi," Timothy said to the young man who answered the door. "We're looking for the little boy who lives here."

The young man looked at them in surprise. He said, "I'm afraid you have the wrong house There's no little boy here."

7
THE RIGHT HOUSE

The cousins could hardly believe their ears. Had they read the address wrong *again*? Was this the right house or wasn't it?

Timothy explained to the man, "This card came to my house—2502—and we figured it was really supposed to go to 2582."

"Well, that's my address," said the man. He took the card that Timothy held out. As soon as he saw the envelope and the card inside, the expression on his face changed. He looked very upset. But it was hard to guess what he was thinking. He said gruffly, "You have the right house. This card is for me."

"*You*?!" cried Timothy. "But—but you're a grown-up!"

The man sighed impatiently. "It's kind of a

joke, OK? Nobody calls me Timmy anymore. But they used to when I was a little boy. And when I was a little boy I used to be crazy about Frosty the Snowman. So—it's just a joke. The card is from someone—someone I used to know, that's all. . . . And why am I explaining all this to you?''

The man started to shut the door. Almost as an afterthought he added, "Uh, thanks for bringing the card. Bye.''

Sarah-Jane said, "It's from your sister.''

Instantly the door flew open. The young man stared at her. "How do you know about Karen? Did she send you here? Because it's no good.''

Titus said, "Nobody sent us here. We cracked the code, that's all. We know it's wrong to read other people's mail. But we thought it was Timothy's mail when we read it.''

Sarah-Jane said, "Do you want to know what the secret message says? It says, '*Forgive me? I come see you? If Yes, bring Frosty's hat. Your sister.*' We're not exactly sure what it means, but that's what it says. We think it means you're supposed to bring a hat to the snowman in the ravine. Do you know where the ravine is? Just go to the return address on the envelope."

All the time Sarah-Jane had been talking, the man had been opening and closing his mouth like a surprised fish. He still couldn't get his words together. Instead, he just waved them away and closed the door.

The three of them glanced at one another. Timothy guessed that his cousins were wondering the same thing he was.

He rang the doorbell again.

The man yanked open the door. "WHAT?"

Timothy said, "Well, aren't you going to do it?"

"Do what?"

"Put a hat on Frosty's head. That's supposed to be the signal. When your sister sees the hat on Frosty's head, she'll know you forgive her. Then you two can be friends again."

The man took a deep breath. "Look. I don't want to be rude. But this is really none of your business. Now, good-bye."

And he closed the door.

None of them felt like ringing the doorbell

one more time. So they turned and headed home.

Titus said, "Did you ever notice that whenever somebody says, 'I don't want to be rude,' they usually go right ahead and are rude?"

Timothy said, "Sisters can drive you crazy, all right. But I wonder what this guy's sister did to make him so mad?"

"Probably nothing," Sarah-Jane sniffed. "It was probably all his fault. And Karen's the nice one who still wants to be friends. But even if she did do something rotten, at least she said she was sorry. If a person says, 'Forgive me?' then the other person should do it. Timmy D. shouldn't go on fighting with Karen. Especially not at Christmas. Especially not when she sent him a cute Christmas card and everything."

Timothy had to admit that Sarah-Jane had a point. He said, "I feel kind of sorry for Karen. I mean, she's going to keep checking her secret snowman to see if her brother brings the hat or not."

Titus said, "Well, maybe Timmy D. will change his mind and bring it."

But Sarah-Jane saw a problem. "Yes, but what if Karen gives up too soon? What if she goes away and stops checking? What if Timmy D. finally brings the hat, but Karen doesn't see it? Then, if she doesn't come to his house—because she didn't see the hat—Timmy D. will think she doesn't want to make up after all. And they'll just go on being mad at each other. Forever!"

Timothy said, "Hey! Maybe *we* could put a hat on Frosty's head. Then at least Karen would know that some people still like her."

Sarah-Jane was so excited by that idea she jumped into a snowbank. She got snow in her boots, which usually she hated. But this time she didn't seem to care. "What a great idea!" Then she frowned. "But I wonder if it can be any old hat or if it has to be like the top hat on the Christmas card?"

"Then how can we do it?" asked Timothy. "Where are we going to get a top hat like that?"

Titus said, "I sort of know how to make one."

"What?" cried Timothy and Sarah-Jane together. "How do you know how to make one?"

Titus explained. "Last year, I was Abraham Lincoln in this play my class put on. My mom and I got a costume book from the library that showed how to make a top hat out of black construction paper."

They didn't have any black construction paper. But Timothy's mother had some red and green for her kindergarten Sunday school class, and she said they could have some.

So they made a very nice green top hat with red trim.

Titus wanted to make a beard, since he knew how to do that, too. But Timothy and Sarah-Jane talked him out of it. They said the snowman didn't really need a beard. And besides, there was no time to lose. They had to get back to the ravine.

8
KAREN

They placed the construction paper hat on the snowman and stood back to admire him. Then they hid behind some bushes to see what would happen.

After what seemed like a long time, they saw someone coming.

A lady with a dog came down into the ravine. She went straight to the secret snowman and took off his hat. She looked at it closely as if she couldn't figure out what was going on.

Sarah-Jane whispered to the boys, "That's the same lady we saw before! Is that Karen?"

Titus whispered back, "It might be. If Timmy D. is a grown-up, probably his sister is, too."

"Well," whispered Timothy. "There's only one way to find out."

He stood up and stepped out from the bushes. Titus and Sarah-Jane scrambled after him.

Timothy called, "Karen! Karen! Wait up!"

Instantly the young woman whirled around. She said, "Aren't you the kids who were here earlier?"

"Yes, I'm Timothy Dawson. And these are my cousins, Sarah-Jane Cooper and Titus McKay."

"I'm very pleased to meet you," said the lady. "But—but how did you know my name?"

It took awhile, but the cousins explained about getting the card by mistake, cracking the code, and seeing Timmy D.

"So you put this paper hat here?" Karen asked.

"Yes," said Timothy. "To show you that some people still like you."

Karen looked like she was going to cry. "Oh, that's so sweet! I'm sorry I tried to chase you away earlier."

"*You*?!" exploded Sarah-Jane. "*You* were the one who threw those snowballs?"

Karen cleared her throat and stooped to untangle the dog's leash from a bush. Timothy thought she might be trying not to laugh, but he wasn't sure. Karen said, "I'm sorry, Sarah-Jane. I didn't know what else to do. You see, I thought you were just some kids playing around. I didn't want anyone to mess with my snowman. I hid it so that only my brother would find it." She stood up. "More than anything else, I wanted to make peace with him."

Sarah-Jane put her hands on her hips and said sternly, "Throwing snowballs at a person is not a peaceful thing to do."

Titus changed the subject. Fast. He said to Karen, "So how come you sent the card and everything? Why not just call your brother up?"

Karen smiled sadly. "I didn't know how he would react. I thought if he got a reminder of how nice things were when we were kids that he would want to be friends again. There weren't a lot of kids around when we were growing up, so Timmy and I played together a lot. He was my little brother, and I kind of took care of him. His full name is Timothy David O'Brien. But I

40

just called him Timmy D. I think brothers and sisters should take care of each other, don't you?"

Timothy nodded.

Sarah-Jane was through being mad about the snowballs. She said, "Tim's the only one of us who has a baby sister. He's luck-ee."

Karen smiled at her. "Anyway, Timmy's favorite song was 'Frosty the Snowman.' We had to sing it all the time—even in the summer. But in the winter we were really lucky, because we had this neat old top hat that our grandfather gave us. We used it every year for our snowmen. Timmy still has it. That's why I asked him to bring it—for old time's sake."

Sarah-Jane asked, "Is that why you sent a message in code? Did you used to do that, too?"

"Yes," said Karen. "And you kids were really smart to figure it out."

"That's because we're the T.C.D.C.," said Titus.

Karen asked, "What's a 'teesy-deesy'?"

"It's letters," Timothy explained.

"Capital T.

Capital C.

Capital D.

Captial C.

It stands for the Three Cousins Detective Club."

Karen said, "Well, I'm sure the T.C.D.C. is great at solving mysteries, but I'm afraid not even you can solve my problem. Almost a year ago, my brother and I had a terrible quarrel."

"That's OK," said Timothy, feeling very grown-up himself. "You don't have to tell us about it. It's private."

Karen nodded gratefully. "Yes. Let's just say we had a quarrel. That was almost a year ago. And we haven't seen each other or even spoken since. I knew I couldn't let Christmas go by without at least trying to make peace.

"A friend asked me to visit. And since I was staying in Timmy's neighborhood, I thought of the snowman idea. I sent the card, built the snowman, and came back here again and again to check for the hat.

"I thought the mail might be slow because of

Christmas, but I never thought of the card going to the wrong house. I'll have to practice making my *eights* better!''

She laughed, but Timothy could tell she was still unhappy.

"It was a good plan," he said to cheer her up.

Karen sighed. "Yes, it was a good plan. Too bad it didn't work."

The cousins were sad, too. They were afraid Karen was right, and they didn't know what to say. Just then, something came rolling down the ravine and bumped into them.

"Oh, no!" wailed Sarah-Jane. "Not another snowball!"

But it wasn't a snowball.

It was a big, black top hat.

9
PEACEMAKERS

The cousins and Karen turned to see Timmy D. hurrying down the ravine toward them. He didn't even get to the bottom, because Karen ran to meet him halfway. They were laughing and crying and talking and hugging all at the same time.

It was nice to see, but it was also a little embarrassing. The cousins wished they could just slip away home. But Karen had handed them the dog leash. So they couldn't exactly leave.

Fortunately, the dog started jumping and barking, because he wanted to be in on the excitement. When Karen and Timmy D. heard the dog barking, they came running over.

Karen said to the cousins, "I want to thank you for being so nice to me."

Timmy said, "And I want to apologize for being so mean to you. Karen's card hit me right out of the blue. I felt so ashamed of myself. A fight is never just one person's fault. It was also my fault that we hadn't spoken for almost a year. Karen asked me to forgive her. But I needed to ask her to forgive *me*, too. Anyway, I was ashamed of myself, and sometimes that makes you act crabby. I'm sorry. If it hadn't been for you kids, I might not have come today."

"Yes," said Karen. "And if it hadn't been for you kids, I might not have waited around."

Timmy D. smiled at them. And when he did, he looked a lot like Karen. He said, "You three are peacemakers. And 'Blessed are the peacemakers, for they will be called the children of God.'"

Timothy recognized that as one of Jesus' Beatitudes. And suddenly he felt as if Jesus Himself had said it right to him. He felt as warm and happy as if he had just drunk a hundred cups of hot chocolate.

"Let's go home and get some hot chocolate," said Sarah-Jane and Titus as if they had read Timothy's mind.

When the cousins got home, Priscilla was up from her nap, cruising around the living room.

Titus said, "Aunt Sarah, did it happen yet? Did Priscilla walk by herself?"

"No, not yet," said Timothy's mother.

"Anytime now," said Sarah-Jane.

Without stopping to take off his jacket, Timothy dropped to his knees. He pulled off his mittens and clapped to Priscilla. "Come on, kid! You can do it!"

Priscilla squealed with delight.

Timothy held out his arms.

And Priscilla let go and toddled straight to her big brother.

The End